★ American Girl

Nanea™

Real Stories **From My Time**

PEARL HARBOR

WITHDRAWN

By Jennifer Swanson

With Nanea Stories by Kirby Larson

Illustrated by Kelley McMorris

Scholastic Inc.

To the men and women who lost their lives in the Pearl Harbor attack on December 7, 1941

Published by Scholastic Inc., *Publishers since 1920*. SCHOLASTIC and associated logos are trademarks and/or registered trademarks of Scholastic Inc. The publisher does not have any control over and does not assume any responsibility for author or third-party websites or their content.

Special thanks to Dr. Derek Frisby

Photos ©: back cover: Library of Congress; 3: Peter Hermes Furian/Alamy Stock Photo; 4: Historical/Getty Images; 12: Hawaiian Historical Society; 15: Chronicle of World History/Alamy Stock Photo; 17: CPA Media-Pictures from History/The Granger Collection; 24: The Granger Collection; 34: AFP/Stringer/Getty Images; 37: TopFoto/The Image Works; 43: Courtesy Nicholson family; 44: Library of Congress; 52: Library of Congress; 56: Associated Press/AP Images; 66: National Archives and Records Administration; 67: Bettmann/Getty Images; 71: Associated Press/AP Images; 78: Myron Davis/Getty Images; 82: Associated Press/AP Images; 83: Everett Collection Historical/Alamy Stock Photo; 92: Pacific Stock/First Light; 93: Associated Press/AP Images.

Illustrated by Kelley McMorris
Book design by Suzanne M. LaGasa

© 2018 American Girl. All American Girl marks, Nanea™, and Nanea Mitchell™ are trademarks of American Girl. Used under license by Scholastic Inc.

americangirl.com/service

ISBN 978-1-338-14894-7

10 9 8 7 6 5 4 3 2 1   18 19 20 21 22

Printed in the U.S.A.   23   First printing 2018

America's past is filled with stories of courage, adventure, tragedy, and hope. The Real Stories From My Time series pairs American Girl's beloved historical characters with true stories of pivotal events in American history. As you travel back in time to discover America's amazing past, these characters share their own incredible tales with you.

CONTENTS

Chapter 1

Island Paradise

When most people think of Hawaii, they picture a lush, tropical island with miles of sandy beaches and palm trees swaying in the warm breeze—and that picture is pretty accurate! But that's only part of Hawaii's beauty. The islands are also home to majestic mountains, crashing waterfalls, tropical rain forests, and ancient volcanoes. With warm temperatures and sunny skies throughout the year, Hawaii is a beautiful place to live and a great place to take a vacation!

Hawaii is not just a beautiful place—the people who live there are warm and welcoming, too. The Hawaiians' attitude toward others is called the **aloha** spirit. The word *aloha* means many things: hello, goodbye, love, affection. The aloha spirit is about showing kindness and respect to one another and accepting differences. It means treating others with care and compassion. In fact, today, Hawaii's nickname is the Aloha State.

Hawaii is an **archipelago**, or a group of islands, spread out across the Pacific Ocean to the southwest of the United States mainland. There are 132 islands, but just seven of them contain most of the population: Niihau, Kauai, Oahu, Maui, Molokai, Lanai, and the Big Island of Hawaii. Although these islands are close to one another, they are fairly **isolated** from the rest of the world. This means that they do not have any nearby neighbors. The largest islands' closest US neighbor is California, which is over 2,300 miles away.

Hawaii's location, about halfway between the US and Asia, made it the perfect spot for a US naval base. Ships stationed there could protect the mainland United States from military threats. In 1900, Hawaii wasn't an American state, but it was a US territory. That meant that the US military could build a naval station in Hawaii. In 1908, the island

The Hawaiian islands

of Oahu became home to Naval Station Pearl Harbor. Having a base in Hawaii allowed the US to refuel their ships on the way to Asia, making a journey across the Pacific Ocean much easier.

By 1940, World War II (WWII) was raging in Europe and Asia—but the US was not involved in the war. Because of Pearl Harbor, islanders were used to planes flying overhead, practicing maneuvers, but the actual war felt far away for them. It was a surprise to most Hawaiians when the war flew right to their own backyard.

An aerial photo of Pearl Harbor before WWII

In 1941, Nanea Mitchell was a nine-year-old girl growing up in Honolulu, Hawaii. Nanea swam in the clear, turquoise-colored water and ran barefoot on the beach with her friends, Lily and Donna. She hiked steep mountain trails with her big brother, David, fished with her dad, and grew flowers in the garden with her mom. Nanea and her older sister, Mary Lou, danced in the backyard, practicing hula or pretending to jitterbug. Wherever Nanea was, she drank in the beauty of her wide-open island life.

Nanea adored her **ʻohana**—her family. She could walk to her grandparents' house. She loved talking with her **tutu kane** (grandfather), who told Nanea stories of what the island was like long ago. She also loved taking hula lessons from her **tutu** (grandmother), a master teacher who had taken lessons from her own mother. Nanea felt honored to carry on tradition that had been part of her family for generations.

Nanea's sense of family extended beyond her relatives. She thought of her friends and neighbors as part of her 'ohana. As islanders, everyone was connected. They helped one another, celebrated joys together, and shared one another's sorrows. This was the way of aloha.

On December 7, 1941, when Nanea's world changed dramatically, her understanding of aloha was more important than ever. Though Nanea is a fictional character, her story will help you imagine what it was like to live through the attack on Pearl Harbor.

Nanea's Story

Rose Momi has been my next-door neighbor for so long that she is part of my ohana—my family. I call her Auntie Rose, and so do my friends Lily and Donna. Auntie Rose makes beautiful **lei**, which she sells to the tourists on the pier. Today, Lily, Donna, and I are on Auntie Rose's back porch, surrounded by baskets of plumeria blossoms.

I've made plenty of lei in hula class, but Donna hasn't. When Auntie Rose offered to teach her, Lily and I asked if we could sit in on the lesson.

Auntie Rose gives us each a basket of flowers, along with a needle and crochet thread.

"Slide your needle through the eye of the bloom," Auntie Rose tells Donna, showing her what to do. As we work, Auntie Rose tells us what it was like to grow up on Oahu when she was a girl and how she learned to make lei from her tutu.

"One of my favorite things about Hawaii is that people take time to talk," Donna says.

"We've all grown up talking story," I say. Lily nods in agreement.

"Our ancestors didn't write down their stories," Auntie Rose explains. "They told them to one another. Talking story keeps our past alive. And taking time to talk story helps us get to really know one another. It helps us really care about our friends and neighbors. It is the way of aloha."

"Well, I like it," Donna says. "When I'm your age, Auntie Rose, I'm going to talk story to my children and grandchildren about living in Honolulu." She holds up her tattered lei. "But I might skip the part about how bad I am at doing *this*!"

"There is a lot of aloha, a lot of love, in that lei," Auntie Rose says, smiling at Donna.

Donna giggles. "Maybe aloha makes up for the lumps."

Chapter 2

The Melting Pot

Hawaii has one of the most **diverse**—or mixed—populations in the world. Over the years, people from many different countries have settled on the islands, bringing their own cultural and ethnic traditions. As a result, Hawaii is a tapestry of different languages, clothing, food, and celebrations.

The first people to settle on the islands were Polynesians. They came from various islands scattered throughout the Pacific Ocean, from New Zealand (near Australia) to Easter Island (near South America). It is believed that the first Polynesians who lived on Hawaii came from the Marquesas Islands, over 2,300 miles away. They made the trip in large canoes between 300 and 600 CE. The Polynesians brought food, livestock, clothing, and plants with them. They landed on the Big Island of Hawaii and built homes and temples. As the population grew, the people spread out, settling on six other nearby islands.

An illustration of early Polynesian settlers

The Polynesians lived simply. They fished for food, planted small crops, and relied on the land to produce what they needed. They also relied on one another. Family—'ohana—was important because everyone helped each other out. A person's 'ohana included more than her blood relatives. The whole community was 'ohana. These close connections helped people survive, and it shaped the way they treated others—with care and compassion. This became the way of aloha and, with the strength of 'ohana, became the core of their culture.

For hundreds of years, settlers to the islands had very little contact with the outside world. That changed in 1778 when English explorer Captain James Cook landed on Kauai. Cook's "discovery" of the islands made the whole world aware of Hawaii. More and more people traveled to see the beautiful islands. Hawaii became a busy seaport for many ships sailing between North America and Asia.

By the early 1800s, American business-men discovered that the rich soil and warm climate of Hawaii was perfect for growing valuable crops, such as sugarcane, pineapple, and coffee. People from the United States moved to Hawaii to build huge plantations for these crops. Over the next sixty years, more than four hundred thousand immi-grants came to Hawaii to work on the plantations. They came from countries like China, Japan, and Portugal, where job opportunities were limited. Plantation work in Hawaii was physically demanding— especially for the children who helped in the fields. Ten-year-old Haruno Nunogawa Sato came to Hawaii from Japan with her family. Haruno helped her father load the sugarcane onto other plantation workers' shoulders so they could carry it to the trucks. During the hottest time of the day she brought heavy cans filled with water from nearby ditches to the workers in the field. When she got older, Haruno dug endless rows for planting sugarcane. It was a hot, dirty job that paid just thirty-five cents a day. Workers started at 4:00 a.m. and worked twelve hour days, six days a week.

The people who came to Hawaii from other countries did not all work on plantations. Some opened shops and businesses. Some

Japanese immigrant workers at a sugarcane field in Hawaii, circa 1885

became teachers or journalists. Some went into politics. They built homes, had families, and joined communities. Their clothing, food, and traditions became part of the local island culture.

The Japanese, for example, introduced mochi, a sticky, sweet rice cake that became a favorite treat in Hawaii. People from the Philippines made food dishes such as longaniza (pork sausage with rice) and pinakbet (eggplant, okra, and tomatoes) popular on the islands. Portuguese food also became common throughout the islands. People of all different ethnicities ate malasadas (doughnuts), pao doce (sweet bread), and Portuguese sausage. And while many people associate the ukulele, a small guitar-like instrument, with Hawaii, it actually originated in Portugal. Hawaiian king Kalakaua requested ukulele music be played at royal gatherings in the 1880s, and shortly thereafter it became a common instrument used in music for the hula dance.

King Kalakaua

As more and more people moved to Hawaii, the ethnic mix on the islands changed. In 1853, Native Hawaiians made up 97 percent of the islands' population. But by 1923, that number was just 16 percent. By 1940, more than ten different ethnic groups were officially recognized as part of the Hawaiian population: Native Hawaiian, Japanese, Chinese, Filipino, Caucasian, Korean, African American, Portuguese, Puerto Rican, and Samoan. With such diversity, people often married someone whose ethnic background was different from their own. That meant their children were of mixed race. Being Hawaiian meant something different for everyone. A child might be part Japanese, part Filipino, part Portuguese, part English, and part Native Hawaiian. Regardless of her ethnic mix, if she could trace any part of her ancestry to the early Polynesian settlers, she considered herself Hawaiian.

The wide range of ethnicities on the island made it the diverse place it is today. The original Hawaiian culture changed over time, but it did not disappear. The spirit of aloha remained strong. Respecting differences and showing kindness continues to be key to being Hawaiian.

Nanea's Story

"Komo mai, welcome!" I call to Lily and Donna as I open the door.

Lily Suda smiles and makes a small bow. She's my oldest friend, and our parents and brothers and sisters do everything together. We are part of the same 'ohana. I call Lily's parents Uncle Fudge and Auntie Betty, and Lily calls my parents Uncle Richard and Auntie May.

That's one of the best things about living in Hawaii. The islands are like a jigsaw puzzle where people of all different shapes and colors fit together. There are people from Japan, like Auntie Betty and Uncle Fudge, and from Portugal, like our mailman Mr. Cruz, and from China, like Mrs. Lin, who has a tiny crack seed shop.

mmm, her dried fruits are the best! And of course there are people from the mainland like Papa and Donna's family.

Behind Lily, Donna Hill blows a big bubble with her gum. Donna's family moved from San Francisco three years ago so her father could work in the Pearl Harbor shipyard, just like Papa. On the first day of first grade, Donna walked right up to me and Lily and said, "Hi! What are your names?" After school, she gave us each a piece of her favorite bubble gum. That was the beginning of our friendship.

Now Donna stops chewing her gum. "Do I smell guava bread?" she asks.

Lily and I laugh. When her family first arrived in Honolulu, Donna didn't want to try any new foods. But she changed her mind pretty fast. She took one tiny bite of Auntie Betty's sweet rice mochi, and then she gobbled up the rest. It was the same with Portuguese sausages and the fresh ahi tuna that Uncle Fudge caught. But Donna's favorite food in Hawaii is Mom's guava bread.

I grin. "My mom baked two loaves this morning. Come on in."

Chapter 3

Celebrations and Negotiations

Because people had immigrated to Hawaii from all over the world, the islands were home to a wide variety of cultural celebrations. Islanders learned the customs of their friends and neighbors, and they celebrated along with them. People of all ethnicities celebrated Chinese New Year, Hinamatsuri (or Girls' Day) for Japan, and attended **luaus**. A luau is a traditional Hawaiian celebration. It marks a special occasion, such as a child's first birthday, a wedding, or a graduation. People

Native Hawaiian hula dancers at a luau in 1938

at a luau enjoy traditional Hawaiian dishes such as poi, a dish made from the root of the taro plant; pork made in an imu (underground oven); and fresh seafood. Entertainment at a luau features traditional Hawaiian music as well as hula dancing.

The respect and acceptance of different cultures is part of the spirit of aloha. In fact, a special celebration known as Lei Day was created in 1927. The lei, a handmade garland of flowers, leaves, shells, or feathers, is the symbol of aloha. Islanders take great care in gathering materials and weaving each lei. They believe the mana, or spirit, of the person who created it is woven into the lei. When the lei is given to someone else, the creator is giving a piece of him- or herself. It is a sign of family, togetherness, and acceptance.

Despite the aloha spirit on the islands, World War II was still being fought on the other side of the world. The Allied forces of England and France were fiercely battling Germany, Italy, and Japan, the Axis powers. The United States government did not want to enter the war, but they were not getting along with the Japanese government.

Japan was a small yet mighty country. Its population and economy were growing. In 1937, Japan invaded China and declared war. The United States government did not want to go to war with Japan, but they wanted to help China. By 1940, the US decided they would not buy goods that Japan was selling, and they wouldn't sell Japan gasoline, oil, or steel. The United States hoped that by cutting off money and important supplies, they could persuade Japan to leave China alone. This made the Japanese government very angry. The US and Japan tried to **negotiate**, or talk, to fix the problem. But since Japan was still trying to take over land from China, the US continued to refuse to buy goods from or sell to Japan.

As the relationship between the US and Japan grew more tense, the US Navy sent a large fleet of ships from Southern California to Pearl Harbor, Hawaii. This gave the navy a better position to send ships into the Pacific if they were needed to defend the West Coast of the US.

Japan saw these economic and military

moves as a threat. Japan's new army minister, General Hideki Tojo, wanted to take action against the United States. What exactly would that action be? Who would be affected? Were these two countries headed for war?

Nanea's Story

After Thanksgiving dinner, Lily and Donna and I take turns washing, rinsing, and drying the dishes. There is a pile of plates and so many pots and pans, but we don't mind. We're having fun laughing and telling jokes. I can hear the adults in the living room until their voices go quiet. I tiptoe across the kitchen and lean against the doorway to listen.

"The negotiations with the Japanese aren't going well," Donna's dad says.

"They have to!" Mom insists. "If they don't..." But her voice just trails off.

"It would be madness if the Japanese didn't cooperate," Tutu Kane says.

"I'm worried," says Lily's father.

Oh no, I think. *They're talking about the war.*

"Everything will be fine," Lily's mother says.

"But if negotiations are going badly, I'm not sure we'll be able to stay out of the fight," Donna's dad replies.

"The diplomats will work things out," Mom says confidently. "The last thing Japan wants is a war with the United States."

I hurry back to the sink and start scrubbing the last dirty pot extra hard. "Did you hear all that?" I whisper to Lily and Donna.

"What? About the war?" Donna blows a bubble and snaps it. "I don't listen to any of that."

But Lily is curious. "What about it?" she asks.

I give the pot one last scrub. *Should I tell them that Uncle Fudge is worried?* I wonder. But grown-ups worry all the time about stuff that doesn't happen.

I let the water out of the sink. "Nothing," I reply, repeating what Lily's mom said. "Everything will be fine."

Chapter 4

A Daring Plan

The time had come for action. General Tojo worked with Admiral Isoroku Yamamoto to plan an attack against the United States. And the target? Hawaii! It was the closest US territory to Japan. More importantly, Honolulu was home to Pearl Harbor as well as a US airbase, Hickam Field. The plan was to destroy the battleships, aircraft carriers, and planes at Pearl Harbor. It would take weeks for the US Navy to send ships from California to fight back. During that

33

time, the Japanese Navy would have full control over the Pacific Ocean.

In order to plan an attack, Admiral Yamamoto needed details about Pearl Harbor. He needed a spy. Takeo Yoshikawa was one of several Japanese spies in Hawaii. Yoshikawa climbed the slopes of a mountain where he had a bird's-eye view of Pearl Harbor

Japanese general Hideki Tojo

and the nearby airfields. He also kept watch at a nearby teahouse. He memorized every ship's name and its location, as well as the number and location of the planes. He sent all this information to Admiral Yamamoto via coded messages.

Now Yamamoto knew exactly where every ship in Pearl Harbor was. He also knew that Sunday was the best day for an attack because fewer sailors were on duty that day of the week. Even with all this information, Yamamoto knew he would need perfect timing to achieve the complete surprise he wanted. What he didn't count on was the brand-new technology in place at Pearl Harbor, called **radar**.

Radar, or **ra**dio **d**etecting **a**nd **r**anging, is a way of detecting objects in the air or water. At the time, radar was still quite new and not very accurate. An operator could tell how far away the object was and what direction it was heading, but not what the object was.

Radar was only an effective warning system if someone was constantly watching for blips to appear or disappear. But in 1941, the radar at Pearl Harbor was not manned all day and night. It was only turned on and monitored for three hours each day, from 4:00 a.m. to 7:00 a.m.

By chance, the two soldiers at the radar outpost station on the morning of December 7, 1941, were late shutting it down. At 7:02 a.m., Private George Elliott noticed a huge blip about 130 miles offshore. He told Private Joe Lockard, who was working with him. The blip was so large that they thought the radar might not be working correctly. They called their superior, who told them to ignore the blip. He believed it was most likely a group of US bomber planes that were expected to fly in shortly. Even though he'd been told to shut down the radar, Private Elliott kept it on a few minutes longer. He wanted more practice

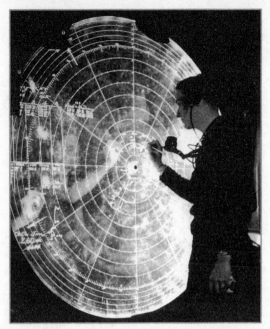

A US Navy technician in the radar room of an aircraft carrier

tracking objects. Private Elliott continued to track the huge blip until it reached 22 miles offshore. Then the large blip disappeared behind a mountain and could no longer be tracked. At 7:39 a.m., Elliott and Lockard shut down the radar station, as ordered.

That blip was actually a massive fleet of Japanese fighter planes. And they were headed straight toward Pearl Harbor!

Nanea's Story

I get up early on Sunday morning so that I can make everything look perfect for the surprise breakfast I planned for my family: cold cereal, fresh papaya, and a batch of Auntie Rose's homemade malasadas. The sweet, puffy Portuguese doughnuts are still warm when I place them in the center of the kitchen table. I want to make things fancy, so I pop into the backyard for some flowers from the garden. The early morning air is fresh and clean as I cut some red and pink hibiscus. I smell the delicate yellow blossoms of the ginger plants from Mrs. Lin's garden. They would be pretty on the table, too, and Mrs. Lin never minds sharing. As I snip a handful of ginger blooms, a little zebra dove perches on the fence. I coo back, and we have a cheerful conversation.

Suddenly, there's a loud rumbling sound, and the little bird flies off. It surprised me, too: What is making that racket? When I look up, I see the sky dotted with planes flying in formation. That's nothing new. Planes from Hickam Field fly overhead all the time, practicing maneuvers. But something is different today. Why are they out so early on a Sunday? And why are they flying so low? As one plane dips down, down, down, I see a round red sun on its tail. Those are not American planes. What's going on?

Chapter 5

Surprise Attack!

On Sunday, December 7, 1941, the Honolulu sky was blue and clear. Islanders were sleeping late, attending church services, or relaxing with their families. Without warning, Japanese planes appeared, and bombs began to fall.

Dorinda Makanaõnalani Nicholson was six years old at the time of the attack. She lived in a house close to Pearl Harbor with her parents and baby brother, Ishmael. As her family was sitting down to breakfast that Sunday morning, they heard loud explosions overhead. Dorinda and her family raced outside to see the sky filled with planes. They were dark green with large orange-red disks: Japanese fighter planes! They flew very low, just over the rooftops. Dorinda could feel the hot exhaust from the plane's engines. The roar of the engines muffled the sound of the bullets that struck her house. She looked back to see holes in the roof. The kitchen, where she was just about to have breakfast, was on fire. Dorinda was terrified. Her parents grabbed her and Ishmael and hustled them to the car. They had to get away from Pearl Harbor! As military vehicles and men rushed toward the base, Dorinda's father drove away from it, searching for safety. At the far end of the harbor, he stopped the car.

Dorinda has never forgotten what she saw at that moment. One of the enormous battleships was upside down in the water.

Other ships were burning uncontrollably. Thick black smoke rose into the air, stinging her nose and making her eyes water. The water in the harbor, usually clean and clear, was a fireball as oil leaked from the ships and burned.

Six-year-old Dorinda with her family at their home, just a few hundred yards from Pearl Harbor

Just before 8:00 a.m., 183 Japanese planes descended upon Pearl Harbor. They bombed the US fighter planes that sat unattended on the airfields. They dropped bombs on the ships docked in an area called Battleship Row. The first wave damaged every battleship. The USS *West Virginia* sank and the USS *Oklahoma* exploded and rolled over,

Pearl Harbor on fire after the attack

trapping hundreds of men inside. The USS *Arizona* took a direct hit to its ammunitions compartment, which set off a massive explosion. The ship broke in two and sank in less than fifteen minutes, taking more than 1,100 sailors with it to their deaths.

When it was over, just before 10:00 a.m., more than twenty-one US Navy ships and over 300 planes were damaged or destroyed. The surprise attack killed 2,335 military personnel and wounded another 1,143.

Civilians, or people who are not in the military, were affected as well. More than sixty of them were killed. The attack was felt all around the island. Seventeen-year-old Keiko Nakata was working in her parents' taro patch out in Kahaluu, a small farming community. Even though she was far away from Pearl Harbor, she heard the sounds of gunfire. She thought it was a drill until a bomb dropped into the neighbor's yard.

Children all over the island were huddled together with their families, wondering what was happening. They listened in fear as the planes zoomed overhead. They cringed as earth-shattering explosions ripped through the air. Some even watched in horror as gigantic fireballs surged high into the sky. In less than two hours, the lives of all the people in Hawaii were drastically changed in ways they could never have imagined.

Nanea's Story

I stand frozen in place as one loud boom after another shatters the quiet morning. In the distance, toward Wheeler Airfield, thick columns of oily black punch bruises in the blue sky.

Suddenly, my brother, David, flies out of the house and snatches me back inside. "Wh-wh-what's happening?" I ask. My teeth are chattering.

David carries me to the sofa. "I don't know," he says. Mom is there, and she holds me close as I describe what I saw outside.

Papa switches on the radio.

"It's eight-oh-four a.m., and this is your KGMB announcer, interrupting this program to

recall all army, navy, and marine corps
personnel to duty."

Everyone stays glued to the radio for the
next fifteen minutes while the announcer calls
twice more for military personnel to report to
duty. Then police officers and firefighters are
ordered to report. But there's no explanation for
what I saw.

"I better get to the shipyard," Papa says,
jumping up to get dressed.

"But you're not military," Mom protests.

Papa says, "I'm sure they'll need civilian
workers, too." Papa is a welder at the Pearl
Harbor shipyard. As soon as he's dressed, he
dashes out the door.

I glance at the clock. It's 8:35. My family is supposed to be at the kitchen table now, enjoying the special breakfast I prepared. It seems like hours ago that I cut flowers for the table. I tremble as if I'm sitting in the icebox.

Papa has barely been gone five minutes when another announcer shouts into the microphone. *"This is no maneuver. This is the real McCoy. Enemy airplanes have attacked."*

Chapter 6

An Island on Fire

As the sounds of the Japanese planes faded off into the distance, more loud explosions filled the air. Pearl Harbor was on fire! Damaged ships lay partially submerged in the water. Oil seeping from the engines pooled on top of the water and caught fire, sending huge clouds of black smoke into the air. Thousands of sailors trapped in the wreckage faced the horrifying choice of sinking with their ships or jumping into flame-filled waters. Many who jumped were immediately burned by the oil.

Surrounded by smoke and burning fuel, they struggled to breathe, struggled to stay afloat, struggled to stay alive. Those who were trapped on their ships pounded desperately against thick metal walls, screaming for help, hoping to be heard and rescued before their ships were completely submerged. No one knew if the attack was over or if more planes were on the way.

Three stricken US battleships after the attack

In the midst of the chaos, people rushed to help. Military personnel jumped into small boats, dodging smoke and flames, risking their own lives to pull survivors to safety. Civilians jumped into action, too. One of the most amazing rescues happened aboard the USS *Oklahoma*. A team led by Julio DeCastro, a Honolulu native, worked for twenty-five hours straight. They cut through a compartment on the ship and rescued the men who had been trapped with little air and rising water. All thirty-two sailors made it out alive. They were lucky. Many of the sailors trapped elsewhere on the ship did not survive.

Some of the injured were transported to the hospital on the base, while others went to the USS *Solace*—a fully equipped medical ship that functioned as a hospital at sea. It was docked in the harbor and, incredibly enough, it did not suffer any damage.

On land, ambulances wailed as they rushed people to the hospital. Doctors, nurses, and medics worked furiously, treating broken bones, cuts, bullet wounds, and severe burns. Many of the men were critically injured and needed extensive care. There were so many wounded that they didn't all fit into the base hospital. Some patients were laid out on the lawns outside the hospital. Dining halls and **barracks**, or sleeping quarters, were converted into temporary hospitals.

Five-year-old Jean Lawson was living with her parents at Schofield Barracks. Her father was in the army and stationed at Pearl Harbor. Just like any normal Sunday morning, she was waiting to go to Sunday school. Suddenly, she looked up and saw planes buzzing right over her house. She heard loud clacking noises as empty casings from used gun cartridges fell like hail onto their roof. Her father hurried to his office at the nearby naval base, bullets flying all around him. Jean's mother clutched her in her arms and ran to the barracks for safety. Once inside, Jean, her mother, and her grandmother were herded into a small room along with other women, children, and even a few family pets. A soldier stood guard at the window, rifle in hand. Jean didn't know what was going on, but she knew she was scared. Later that night, Jean, her mother, and her grandmother were packed on a bus and evacuated to a schoolhouse in the hills for safety. Jean eventually left Hawaii with her mother and grandmother.

Within hours of the attack, Hawaiian governor J. B. Poindexter declared a state of emergency. Civilians were ordered to stay in their homes and off the roads. Armed soldiers patrolled the city, keeping the streets clear for military and rescue vehicles. Civilians were also told to stay off the phone so the landlines were clear for military or emergency calls.

Armed soldiers standing guard at Wheeler Field after the attack

Panicked families could not contact loved ones to find out if they were safe.

Desperate for information, the people of Hawaii stayed glued to their radios. There were no televisions, no twenty-four-hour news stations, and no Internet in Hawaii in 1941. Radio was the only source of immediate news. But at 11:41 a.m., almost four hours after the attack began, all the radio stations suddenly went off the air.

The silence made the horror of the attack even worse. Many people kept their radios on, listening to static and waiting for news—any news. Others tuned to the police band, listening to police officers communicate with one another in hopes of getting more information. Rumors quickly spread. People said that the water supply was poisoned, the city of Honolulu was on fire, and Japanese soldiers were hiding in the hills and fields around Pearl Harbor. None of these claims were true, but without any connection to real news, it was impossible to know for sure what was real and what was a rumor.

Scared and confused, islanders listened to the wailing of sirens and ambulances and the rumbling of military vehicles. They waited in their homes, wondering what would happen next. Was there another attack coming?

Nanea's Story

Fire truck sirens howl in the distance, roaring louder and louder. I edge closer to Mom, shivering. I can't stop thinking about what I saw from the backyard, the thick black plumes of smoke smudging the blue, blue sky.

"The radio announcer just told us to fill our bathtubs with water," my sister, Mary Lou, says. "Buckets, too. In case the Japanese cut off our water supply." She dashes to the bathroom.

I sit frozen in front of the radio, afraid to miss another word. The announcer is speaking in his smooth-as-butter voice, as if talking about the price of pineapples or sugar. "Here is a warning to all people through the Territory of

Hawaii and especially the island of Oahu. In the event of an air raid, stay under cover. I repeat. If an air raid should begin, do not go out of doors. Stay under cover."

A sudden rapping at the front door makes me jump a mile. It's Auntie Rose from next door. "Everyone okay?" she asks.

Mom grabs her hand and pulls her inside. "Yes. You?"

"There are a few bullet holes in my kitchen walls," Auntie Rose says in disbelief. "But I'm all right."

Mom's face goes pale, and I just stare at Auntie Rose. Bullet holes? Right next door? I shiver even harder.

But before I can say anything, Mary Lou rushes in. "The bathtub's filled," she announces.

Mom gives her two more buckets. "Fill these, too, please." She brushes her hair back from her face. "I need to gather up blankets to cover the windows. The radio just announced that there will be a blackout tonight." She bustles off without even explaining what a blackout is.

Suddenly, a crackling static fills the room. "What happened to the radio?" I ask.

"KGMB's off the air," Mary Lou says. "KGU, too." She turns the radio dial back and forth, but there's nothing. Not one sound at all.

I feel so afraid that I start to cry.

Chapter 7

Under Military Control

As the day wore on, it was difficult to know what was *really* happening. The fear of the unknown was overwhelming. No one knew if the attacks were over, and everyone wondered if there would be another wave of planes. Would the Japanese invade the island?

At 3:30 p.m., the radio stations came back on the air with the announcement that Hawaii was under **martial law**. Then all stations went off the air again so that the Japanese couldn't use the radio signals to find the islands and return for another attack.

Martial law meant that the military now controlled everything. A new military governor was in charge, and he had the right to put special laws into place that every person living on the islands had to obey. Effective immediately, no one could be outside from 6:30 p.m. to 6:00 a.m. Anyone who was outside during those hours had to have a military pass. Anyone without a pass could be fined or arrested. If someone was visiting friends and didn't leave before 6:30, she'd have to stay at her friend's house all night—and after 6:30, the friends would not be allowed to play outside.

Also effective immediately were nightly blackouts. All windows had to be closed and covered with dark fabric or paper. Streetlights and exterior lights on buildings and businesses had to be off. Very few cars were allowed on the road at night, and any that were had to shield their headlights. All these rules ensured that it was completely dark at night. If enemy planes returned, there wouldn't be any light to help them find the islands. Block wardens patrolled neighborhoods, making sure it was dark. If they found any sign of light, they made sure it was put out. The wardens could even fine those who broke the rules.

Nightly blackouts were difficult and sometimes scary. Islanders who were used to enjoying cool breezes through their open windows now had to spend long hours in their dark, stuffy homes. Most didn't have electric fans. Simple actions, such as taking a bath, eating a meal, or talking to family members were eerie and unsettling in the dark. For many it was a scary and uncomfortable situation that went on night after night: a constant reminder of the horrible attack.

June Yoshida, who was a small child at the time, vividly remembers the nightly blackouts. They were not allowed to use regular light bulbs. Instead, they had to paint the bulbs black except for a small circle on the bottom. The small amount of light that shone through the open area was all that she could use to read her book.

President Franklin D. Roosevelt signing the declaration of war against Japan

After the first blackout, islanders awoke to news. On December 8, 1941, US president Franklin D. Roosevelt formally declared war on Japan. The United States was now involved in World War II. Life changed for all Americans, and especially for those living in Hawaii.

A newspaper headline from the day after the attack

Under martial law, the military controlled every part of daily life in Hawaii. School was immediately canceled, and some school buildings were turned into military hospitals. Students had no idea when classes would start again—if at all. This break from school wasn't like a vacation. Christmas was a few weeks away, but war loomed over the holiday. The ship that was bringing Christmas trees from the mainland turned around after the Japanese attack, so the trees were never delivered. Mandatory blackouts meant shops and homes couldn't display holiday lights.

The military told businesses when they could open and when they had to close. Movie theaters had only two showtimes: noon and 2:00 p.m. Restaurants stopped serving at 4:00 p.m. so workers and customers could get home before the 6:30 curfew. As more and more military people came to Hawaii, there were long lines at restaurants and shops, and public transportation was crowded. People had to plan extra time for their normal, everyday activities. They also had to know where to find a public bomb shelter in case of another attack or an air raid drill. An air raid drill was practice—in case of another attack. When people heard sirens wailing, they ran for shelter. Some ran to a bomb shelter, or to a bunker that gave them shelter. At home, every civilian had a bunker in their yard. Digging a shelter in the ground was another rule of martial law. Everyone had to have a safe place to go if there was an attack.

All communication was **censored**, which meant it was reviewed and sometimes changed. The military took over newspapers, magazines, and radio broadcasts to ensure that only approved information was shared. They controlled the telephone company and monitored calls. The military was afraid that people on the islands might accidentally share information that would help Japan plan another attack. That meant no one was allowed to talk about the weather or discuss anything about the construction or repairs taking place on the islands—especially at Pearl Harbor. Mail was censored, too. That meant that every letter going out of or coming into Hawaii was opened and read—and sometimes changed—before it was delivered.

A few weeks after Pearl Harbor was bombed, everyone in Hawaii over the age of six had to be fingerprinted and carry an identification card. If there was an emergency, people could be properly identified. The military also ordered citizens to carry a gas mask at all times in case the Japanese attacked the islands with poisonous gas. Joan Rodby, who was ten years old at the time, remembers getting her large, uncomfortable gas mask. When her school finally reopened in February 1942, Joan had to take her gas mask with her to her classes. Her school had drills to see how fast the students could put them on. If the air raid siren went off, they needed to have the gas masks on immediately. Breathing poisonous gas, even for a few seconds, would be deadly. Joan, like every other student, hung her gas mask off the back of her desk chair while she was in school. When she left, the gas mask was slung over her arm or hanging from her books. Joan said the gas mask was like having an extra arm with you all the time.

A student is fitted for a gas mask at her school in Honolulu

Military families considered "non-essential" by the government, such as the wives and children of military personnel, were sent to the US mainland. Families and friends were torn apart with no idea of how long they'd be separated. Nearly 30,000 women and children left the island.

Helen Griffith Livermont was thirteen when she was evacuated from Oahu with her mother and sister, leaving her army father behind. Helen left in April 1942, and the ocean liner taking her to the mainland was packed with other women and children who were leaving family and friends behind. The journey was scary. Several armed navy ships traveled alongside the ocean liner as it left Honolulu to keep it safe from the Japanese submarines that were rumored to be in the waters. Helen worried that their ship could be sunk, and she had no idea how long it would be until she saw her father—or Hawaii—again.

Martial law was put in place to make the islands—and the people who lived on them—safe. But the changes were difficult, and they served as constant reminders that Hawaii was an active war zone. The people who lived in Hawaii kept their eyes to the sky, always fearful of more attacks.

Nanea's Story

I'm curled up on the sofa, reading, when Mom announces that it's time to get ready for the blackout.

While she and Mary Lou pull the blankets down over the windows, I go around the house, turning out the few lights that are on. With each button I push, the house grows gloomier. And so do my spirits.

Keeping busy all afternoon kept my mind off my sad feelings. But now that the house is dark, my worries wriggle back in like geckos, over, under, and around. My finger rests on the last light switch. This will be the fifth pitch-black night. The fifth night of staying inside the stuffy, dark house instead of roller skating or playing tag or kick the can.

It will also be the fifth night without Papa. It seems like years since I sat on the porch with him, listening to the trilling crickets and the funny little quacks of the geckos. As the neighbors washed supper dishes, Papa and I would talk about our dreams, plan fishing trips, and tell jokes. The "before" night sky had been soft, twinkling with stars. This "after" nighttime is sharp and lonely.

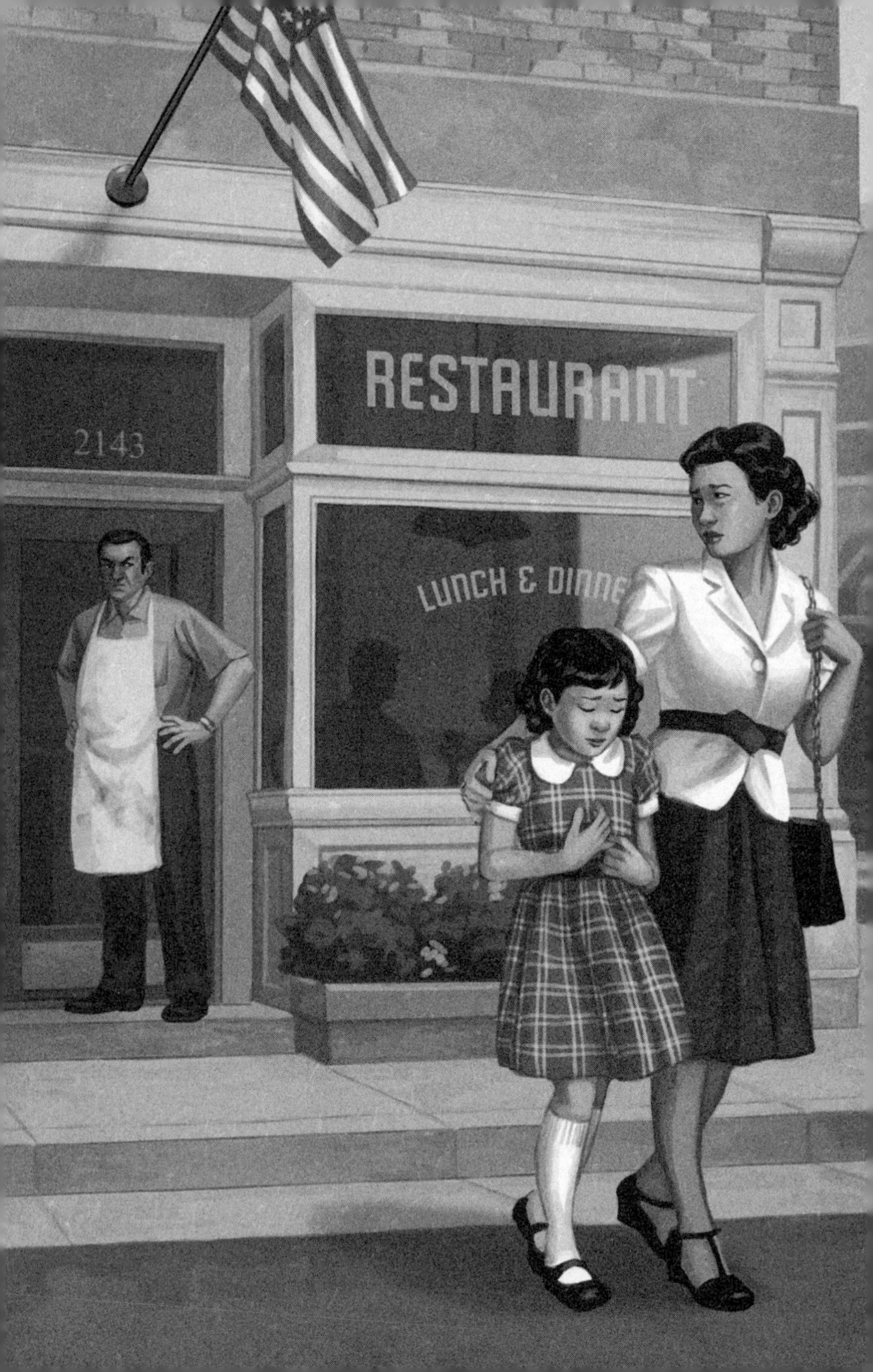
RESTAURANT
2143
LUNCH & DINNE

Chapter 8

Americans of Japanese Ancestry

Martial law was declared on the islands not just to establish control, but also to keep track of the large population of Americans of Japanese Ancestry, or AJAs. Anyone of Japanese descent was treated with suspicion by military leaders, who thought that Americans of Japanese Ancestry would be more loyal to Japan than to America.

The government took immediate steps to prevent AJAs from communicating with Japan. The first few days after the attack, more than four hundred Americans of Japanese Ancestry were arrested. Many of them were legal US citizens. They were all jailed because they were of Japanese descent, not because they had done anything wrong.

Some who were taken into custody by the military were released after a few weeks. Others were held longer—some for four years, until the war ended. Those who remained in

Japanese-American families arriving at an internment camp

custody were sent to **internment camps** and kept against their will.

The suspicion toward AJAs caused tension and fear among islanders with any Japanese heritage. Many worried that a government official would show up on their doorstep and take them or their parents away.

That happened to Ruth Matsuda. Within a few days of the attack on Pearl Harbor, several Federal Bureau of Investigation (FBI) agents came to her house. They were there to take her father away. He owned a respectable trucking company, but because he had been born in Japan, the government was worried he was loyal to his former homeland. It was too risky, the FBI said, to allow Ruth's father to remain free. Ruth's father was very ill, and Ruth managed to convince the military not to take him away.

Internment of AJAs was not limited to the islands. Close to 120,000 Americans of

Japanese Ancestory on the mainland United States were forced into internment camps. The interment of AJAs was a violation of their **civil rights**. These rights protect individuals from unfair treatment based on race or ethnicity. The US government ignored the rights of AJAs, believing it was necessary to keep the country safe.

In Hawaii, it was not practical to put all Americans of Japanese Ancestry into internment camps. Almost one-third of the population, more than 158,000 people, had Japanese heritage. There was no one place on the islands large enough to house that many people. Moving them off the islands was not an option. The military did not have the manpower or money to transfer them all to the mainland. Interning so many people would also cause problems for the local economy. People of Japanese ancestry ran shops and businesses. They were plantation workers and fishermen. Their skills were necessary to keep the economy going. Instead, the government chose certain members of the Japanese communities, such as religious leaders, business owners, teachers at Japanese language schools, and editors of Japanese newspapers, and sent them to camps.

AJAs who were not sent to internment camps still faced **discrimination**, or unfair treatment. They had earlier curfews and many travel restrictions. Many had problems being served in restaurants or gas stations. They were not allowed to live close to Pearl Harbor, where they might see military activity and report it to the enemy. If they objected to these rules, they were sent to an internment camp.

To prevent suspicion, many Americans of Japanese Ancestry gave up their Japanese customs. They stopped practicing judo, a Japanese martial art, or attending Japanese language

81

A Japanese family returns from an internment camp to find their home vandalized

school. They didn't display the Japanese flag, wear traditional Japanese clothing, or read books in Japanese—all things they were able to do freely before the war.

Despite the racism they experienced, many American men of Japanese ancestry were eager to defend the United States. They were patriotic and loyal and wanted to join the military. When the war began, Japanese American men over the age of eighteen flocked to recruitment centers to enlist.

They were turned away. The US government classified them as "enemy aliens" and refused to allow them to serve.

Two years into the war, in 1943, the US needed more soldiers. The military ban against AJAs was lifted. President Franklin D. Roosevelt supported the end of the ban, saying, "Americanism is a matter of the mind

A Japanese American soldier is awarded the Bronze Star Medal for heroism in 1945

and heart; Americanism is not, and never was, a matter of race or ancestry." When the army called for 1,500 new volunteers in Hawaii, more than 9,500 Japanese Americans showed up, eager to prove their loyalty to America.

The Japanese Americans that volunteered became the 100th Infantry Battalion/442nd Regimental Combat team. It was an all Japanese American unit made up mostly of men from Hawaii. The unit fought some of the fiercest, most difficult battles in the war, facing horrible conditions. These brave men were willing to risk their lives for a country that mistrusted and mistreated them.

Nanea's Story

When Donna and I get to Lily's house, Lily is curled up on the sofa, crying. Four days ago, when Pearl Harbor was attacked, Lily's father was taken away by the FBI. I saw it happen. Two men in dark suits led Lily's dad to a car parked at the curb. They looked like mobsters from a movie. Lily had pleaded with the men. "Please don't take my daddy!" she'd screamed. It was awful.

I look at Lily now. Her eyes are puffy and red-rimmed. "Maybe now isn't a good time?" I ask.

Lily wipes her eyes. "No, I'm glad you're here," she says.

As I sit down next to Lily, Donna says, "Hey,

where's your radio? It's always right there by the sofa."

Lily pauses. "We had to turn it in to the police."

"What for?" Donna asks.

"Is that another new rule?" I sigh. I wonder if my family will have to give up our radio, too.

Lily shakes her head. "Only for us."

"I don't understand," Donna says, sitting on the other side of Lily. ""Us?"

In a tiny voice, Lily answers, "Because we're Japanese."

"But you're loyal Americans!" I say. "Your family has lived here forever!"

A tear plops on Lily's lap. "Last night, my

brother came out of work and someone had written in soap on his windshield. It said, 'Go home, Jap.'"

I gasp. "That's terrible."

"I'd like to find the person who wrote that and sock him in the nose." Donna makes a fist with her hand. *"Pow."*

Lily laughs a little, although it's a sad laugh. "You might have to sock a lot of people. It's not easy to be Japanese right now," she says. "I really wish Daddy was here."

This war is wrecking everything, I think.

Chapter 9

Kokua

On December 7, 1941, when Governor Poindexter declared a state of emergency, he asked the people of Hawaii to be willing to help in any way they could. Islanders—including children—responded immediately, volunteering to help in many ways. Their willingness to help was rooted in **kokua**. Kokua means "assistance" or "a good deed." Helping others is part of the culture of Hawaii, and islanders do so without expecting reward or praise. Kokua had always been important to the people of Hawaii, but now, it was more important than ever.

The day after the attack, children from church groups, Girls Scouts, Boy Scouts, and the Junior Red Cross showed up to work. They went to hospitals, first-aid stations, evacuation centers, canteens, and offices. Girls and boys ran errands and delivered supplies. They cooked, served food, and cleaned up for aid workers and volunteers in evacuation centers.

As the war went on, children, teenagers, and college students continued to help when and where they were needed. Older children looked after younger children when mothers volunteered for the war effort. Kids made homemade cards and cookies for the wounded soldiers in Hawaii. They knitted sweaters and socks for members of the military stationed around the world. Some high school and college students went to work at plantations, picking pineapples and sugar-cane. Others worked in offices, factories, or even for the military.

Children of all ages helped at the United Service Organizations (USO). The USO provided entertainment and relaxation to those serving in the armed forces. Civilians put on shows, dances, and dinners to help boost morale and get people's minds off the war.

A group of Japanese American college students who were refused enrollment in the army still wanted to help with the war effort. They formed the Varsity Victory Volunteers. These young men helped rebuild the Schofield Barracks, which were destroyed during the attack on Pearl Harbor. They dug ditches, built roads, and worked in the quarries to get stone for buildings. With so many other men heading off to war, there was a desperate need for people to perform demanding physical tasks.

Throughout the war, there were many injured military men on the island, there was a constant need for blood. Many people were willing to donate blood, but the Red Cross desperately needed bottles for storage. So volunteers, many of them children, organized drives and collected bottles.

Regardless of how they helped, many young people worked long hours, continuing to volunteer even after school was back in

The Varsity Victory Volunteers help with war effort, circa 1943

Students are taught first aid at school during a drill in Honolulu

session. They kept up with their studies and supported the war effort. Their dedication and hard work stemmed from their sense of aloha and their deeply held belief in kokua. As they took on grown-up responsibilities, their experiences changed their carefree island way of life forever.

Nanea's Story

"What are you doing?" calls Lily as we walk over to Auntie Rose's yard.

"Is that dye?" Donna asks.

Auntie Rose nods. "Now that the tourists have stopped coming, we lei sellers don't have any customers. But Uncle Sam has decided to use our sewing skills for making camouflage netting." She smiles proudly. "Now we are as busy as ever."

"What does the government want with camouflage nets?" Donna asks.

"They'll use them to cover buildings and equipment and even soldiers," Auntie Rose explains.

"That way, enemy planes can't see them from the air."

"Can we help?" I ask Auntie Rose.

"Of course," Auntie Rose says. She hands each of us a stout stirring stick and shows us what to do.

I'm in front of a tub filled with olive-green-colored water. I start stirring the murky liquid in a figure-eight pattern, just like Auntie Rose showed us. Donna stirs brown, and Lily black. We stir and stir and stir.

Auntie Rose carefully fishes out the wet fabric pieces and hangs them on shrubs around her yard so they can dry.

"One more step," she says. Auntie Rose begins to tear lengths of dry fabric into strips, and then the strips into smaller bits. "I'll weave these strips into the netting," she explains.

"This is easier than stirring," Lily says, ripping a strip of fabric in half.

I tear the pieces as fast as I can. "Oops!" I hold up a tiny scrap. "This one's too small. I'd better throw it away."

Auntie Rose stops me. "Good nets are made with lots of different fabric scraps. All shapes. All sizes. No piece is too small."

My heart flutters happily. No piece is too small. That means no helper is too small.

Epilogue

For months after the bombing of Pearl Harbor, the citizens of Hawaii lived in fear of another attack. That changed in June of 1942, when American forces defeated the Japanese at Midway Island. The Battle of Midway was not the end of the war, but it was an important victory. Hawaii was no longer in constant danger of additional Japanese attacks, since the Japanese ships were no longer close by. Islanders breathed a sigh of relief.

The worries of war and the rules of martial law still existed, but Hawaii felt safer.

World War II ended in 1945. The people of Hawaii were eager to return to normal life, but that wasn't so easy to do. Islanders had been witnesses to war. What they had seen and heard and felt was unforgettable. More than four thousand Americans of Japanese Ancestry had been held in internment camps on the islands. They returned home, but they carried their prison experiences with them. Those who survived the war were forever changed because of it.

Today, the USS *Arizona* still rests at the bottom of the harbor. It is now a national historic landmark, and more than a million people from all over the world visit it each year. They come to pay their respects to the people who gave their lives on that fateful day in history: December 7, 1941.

Glossary

Archipelago — a group of islands

Barracks — a building or group of buildings where soldiers live

Censor — to examine letters, phone calls, books, etc., in order to remove anything considered harmful

Civil rights — the rights every person should have, no matter what his or her race, gender, ethnicity, or religion may be

Civilian — a person who is not a member of the military

Discrimination — when a person or group is treated unfairly, often because of race, gender, or religion

Diverse — made up of things different from one another

Internment camps — areas where many Americans of Japanese Ancestry were forced to stay after the attack on Pearl Harbor, many for years, until World War II ended

Isolated — separate; alone

Martial law — when the military has full control of an area

Negotiate — to discuss in order to arrive at an agreement

Radar — a device that uses radio waves to determine the position of a moving object

Hawaiian Terms

Aloha (ah-LO-hah) — can mean hello, goodbye, love, affection. The aloha spirit is about showing kindness and respect to one another and accepting differences.

Kokua (KOH-KOO-ah) — a good deed; helping others without expectation of reward or praise

Lei (LAY) — a handmade garland of flowers, leaves, shells, or feathers

Luau (LOO-ow) — a traditional Hawaiian celebration that marks a special occasion

'Ohana (oh-HAH-nah) — family

Tutu (TOO-too) — grandparent, usually grandmother

Tutu Kane (TOO-too KAH-nay) — grandfather

Source Notes

Allen, Gwenfread. *Hawaii's War Years: 1941–1945*. Honolulu, Hawaii: University of Hawaii Press, 1950.

Bailey, Beth and David Farber. *The First Strange Place: Race and Sex in World War II Hawaii*. Baltimore, Maryland: Johns Hopkins University Press, 1992.

Green, Thomas H. "Martial Law in Hawaii." *Martial Law in Hawaii Dec 7, 1941–April 4, 1943*, 1943, doi: Library of Congress, official military document.

Kimble, James J. *Mobilizing the Home Front: War Bonds and Domestic Propaganda*. College Station, Texas: Texas A&M University Press, 2006.

Lord, Walter. *Day of Infamy*. New York, New York: Henry Holt and Company, 2001.

McKinnon, Shaun. "Attack on the USS Arizona: 14 Minutes and a Lifetime." *Pensacola News Journal*, December 7, 2014. http://www.pnj.com/story/news/military/2014/12/06/uss-arizona-pearl-harbor/19986311/.

Nicholson, Dorinda Makanaōnalani. *Pearl Harbor Child: A Child's View of Pearl Harbor: From Attack to Peace*. Kansas City, Missouri: Woodson House Publishing, 2001.

Nicholson, Dorinda Makanaōnalani. *Remember World War II: Kids Who Survived Tell Their Stories*. Washington, DC: National Geographic Society, 2006.

Oaks, Robert F. *Hawaii: A History of the Big Island*. Charleston, South Carolina: Arcadia Publishing, 2003.

Odo, Franklin. *No Sword to Bury: Japanese Americans in Hawaii During World War II*. Philadelphia, Pennsylvania: Temple University Press, 2004.

Prange, Gordon W. et al. *At Dawn We Slept: The Untold Story of Pearl Harbor*. New York, New York: Penguin Books, 1991.

Richardson, K. D. *Reflections of Pearl Harbor: An Oral History of December 7, 1941*. Westport, Connecticut: Praeger Publishers, 2005.

Rodriggs, Lawrence Reginald. *We Remember Pearl Harbor*. Newark, California: Communications Concepts, 1991.

Rothman, Lily. "Powerful Stories of the Japanese-American Children Who Witnessed Pearl Harbor." *Time* magazine, December 6, 2016. http://www.time.com/4589051/pearl-harbor-children/.

Scheiber, Harry N. and Jane L. Scheiber. *Bayonets in Paradise: Martial Law in Hawaii During World War II.* Honolulu, Hawaii: University of Hawaii Press, 2016.

Tranquada, Jim and John King. *The 'Ukulele: A History.* Honolulu, Hawaii: University of Hawaii Press, 2012.

"A View of Daily Life at Honouliuli Internment Camp. ca. 1945 Photo by R.H. Lodge, Courtesy Hawaii's Plantation Village. Honouliuli Internment Camp." National Park Service, Honolulu, Hawaii. http://www.nps.gov/hono/learn/historyculture/index.htm.

Wohlstetter, Roberta. *Pearl Harbor: Warning and Decision.* Stanford, California: Stanford University Press, 1962.

Wortman, Marc. "The Children of Pearl Harbor." *Smithsonian.com,* Smithsonian Institution, December 5, 2016. http://www.smithsonianmag.com/history/children-pearl-harbor-180961290/.

"WWII Living History Group." *WWII USO Preservation Association.* http://www.ww2uso.org/history.html.

Timeline

1937 – Japan invades China, starting World War II in the Pacific

1939 – Germany invades Poland, starting World War II in Europe

1940 – The United States imposes sanctions and embargoes on Japan

1941, December 7*

> **7:02 a.m.** – Private George Elliott notices an unusual blip on the radar machine
>
> **7:39 a.m.** – Transportation arrives to take the radar operators back to base, and the radar machine is shut down
>
> **7:50 a.m.** – The first wave of Japanese fighter planes begin the attack on Pearl Harbor
>
> **8:06 a.m.** – The USS *Arizona* is hit, killing thousands of men in the explosion

10:00 a.m. – The Japanese planes retreat, leaving destruction and chaos in their wake

10:30 a.m. – Both military personnel and civilians jump into action, taking the injured to the hospital in droves

11:41 a.m. – All radio stations on the islands go silent

3:00 p.m. – Hawaiian governor J. B. Poindexter declares a state of emergency

3:30 p.m. – Radio stations come back on the air briefly to announce that the Hawaiian islands are now under martial law

1941, December 8 – The United States joins World War II by declaring war on Japan

1942 – American forces defeat the Japanese at the Battle of Midway, ending the threat of another attack on the islands

1943 – The US military ban on Americans of Japanese Ancestry is lifted

1945 – Japan formally surrenders, bringing World War II to an end

*Times** for the day of the attack are in local Hawaiian time and in some cases are estimated as closely as possible based on various accounts and military reports.